May your greatness shine!
Sunny Choi
- 2017

written by Laura N. Clement   illustrated by Sunny J. Choi

Egg
Copyright © 2017 by Laura N. Clement
Artwork Copyright © 2017 By Sunny J. Choi

Summary: When you're destined for greatness but can't swim, life in a duck family is a little complicated, especially if you're a dragon who just happens to sneeze, fire. Egg is a hero on her very own journey, slightly out of place and lost in her world but surrounded by love and unknown danger. WHOMPBOOM! along with Egg on her adventure as she discovers sometimes greatness is within you all along.

Clear Fork Publishing
P.O. Box 870
102 S. Swenson
Stamford, Texas 79553
(325)773-5550
www.clearforkpublishing.com

Printed and Bound in the United States of America.

ISBN - 978-1-946101-13-6

Clear Fork Publishing

www.clearforkpublishing.com

To the young, or young at heart on a journey for greatness. Never give up.

To the heart and loves of my life- Mia, Martin, Mom and Dad. Thank you greatly.

To all my good friends, those who have supported me by reading, editing and offering encouragement, especially when things seems darkest, I give my most heartfelt thanks. I could not have done this without you.

For Callie, whose support and love of Egg made this whole adventure possible.

And to Sunny, for her art and friendship. You made the of hatching of Egg joyful. Thank You.

- Laura

To L.Clement, my picture book sister, & CFP for finding me my PB sister.

To J.Chu, my PB fairy god mother, & J+S, my little but tall dragons.

-Sunny

Egg was destined for greatness.

She just needed a little help finding it.

"You're cold!" Mother duck shrieked.
"You need a nest...come with me."

"I'll call you Waddle...
you Willow, and you, Skip."
Her mom paused,
"We'll call you Egg."

No one minded that Egg was... different.
She was unique, even her quack.

Ggguuuawwwccckk!

"Not everyone needs to quack," said her mom,
"or feathers. Your scales and shiny teeth are
something... special."

Even Egg's sneeze was special.

"Wow!" quacked Waddle.

"That's amazing!" whispered Willow.

"And very hot!" snorted Skip.

"Egg!" quacked her mom. "Remember to cover your nose when you sneeze."

Adventures around the farm were always fun,
with lots of exciting places to discover.

Egg's favorite was inside the mailbox.

I wish I had a stamp, she thought with a giggle. *Then I could travel the world!*

Egg loved everything about life on the farm
except for… family pond time.

Each day was an adventure for Egg, full of all
sorts of curiosities.
There was just one thing missing.
Her greatness.

Could it be in there?

Egg searched and searched
but found... nothing.

Pretty soon, she'd explored
the farm, the whole farm,
until there was only one place
left...

The pond.

It took some practice. A lot of practice.
But eventually, Egg learned how to swim.

Not in the water like a duck.
Underwater like a fish.
But even underwater, Egg found... nothing.

Tired of playing hide-and-seek with her greatness, Egg stopped looking.

Everyone tried to cheer her up.

"You're the best swimmer," Willow told her.

"The bravest sister," Waddle quacked.

"With the best sneezes and the warmest hugs." Skip giggled.

"And," said her mom,

"the perfect waddle!"

But nothing helped. Egg didn't feel like the best or the bravest at anything.

Holding her breath forever and swimming on the bottom of the pond, having the perfect waddle, or even sneezing fire was not great. That was just her.

Nothing special.

Until one day…

"My nest is empty! My nest is empty!" squawked a chicken.

"My eggs are MISSING!" shrieked a duck. The farm was in a tizzy.

Egg wanted to help.

That night, surrounded by darkness
and strange noises, Egg sat fidgeting on top of the
highest haystack.

Egg giggled, *I bet I could see everything if I sneezed.*

WHOMPBOOM!

Yes. That helped. And it made her feel brave too. Until... Egg's scales started to itch.

Rrrrraaattttlleeess...

What was that? she wondered.

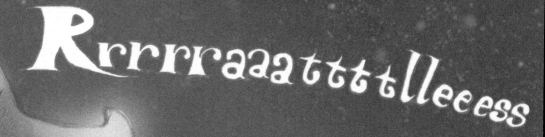

Rrrrraaattttlleeess

Then her nose started
to twitch.

Rrrrraaattttlleeess

And her scales grew
molten hot.

"SNAKE!" Egg shouted

Springing into action,
she dove into the air like a
torpedo with a

WHOMPBOOM!

Fire nipped the snake's nose.

WHOMPBOOM!

And bit its belly.

WHOMPBOOM!

And taunted its tail.

Egg was a blaze of glory, chasing the snake into the forest until it...disappeared.

"He won't be back!" Egg chuckled, stumbling over the missing eggs.

The farm was safe and Egg smiled.

Her greatness had been with her all along.

"Now, about your name," Egg's mom quacked with pride.

"Blayze!" quacked Waddle, "It should be Blayze!"

"Blayze the Amazing!" squeaked Skip.

"Blayze the Invincible!" squealed Willow.

"Blayze, it is," quacked her mom.

"WHOMPBOOM!"

replied Blayze.

Laura N. Clement

Laura is the author of EGG. She was born in Fairbanks, Alaska where her parents gifted her a childhood full of adventure and imaginative opportunities. She currently lives in Seattle with her husband and amazing daughter who are the two best travel buddies an explorer could ever want. A lover and writer of poetry since childhood she continues to explore the myriad of possibilities the imagination can present and abundance of entertaining and soulful character life illuminates.

www.clementcreations.net

Quack!

Sunny J. Choi

"Sunny" Joung Sun Choi is a children's book illustrator currently living in San Francisco. She was born, raised, and studied oriental painting in Korea. She came to San Francisco to study more in children's book illustration and graduated with an MFA in Illustration, and has been a member of Society of Children's Book Writers and Illustrators (SCBWI) ever since.

She works in a flowery cave day and night, lives with two little dragons who sneeze a thunder that startles their tiny dog named Lily.

http://sunnyjchoi.com/

CPSIA information can be obtained
at www.ICGtesting.com
Printed in the USA
BVOW05*2254200617

486850BV00001B/2/P